Pooh's
Sled Ride

A Winnie the Pooh First Reader

Pooh's Sled Ride

Isabel Gaines

ILLUSTRATED BY Studio Orlando

DISNEP
PRESS

NEW YORK

Pooh's
Sled Ride

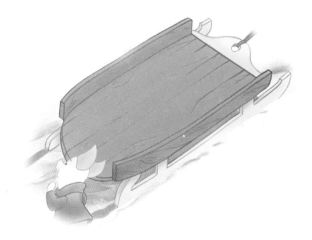

One white winter morning,
Pooh woke up
thinking of sledding.

He went to Owl's house
and said,

"Owl, let's go sledding!"

"A splendid idea!" said Owl.

"I will tell everyone

to meet at the big hill."

Everyone met at the big hill.

"I'm too small to sled,"

said Piglet.

"I always fall off."

"Just hang on to my tail,"
said Tigger.
"You won't fall."

They all piled
onto Christopher Robin's sled.

Piglet hung on to Tigger's tail
at the very back.

13

Down, down they went.

"Wee!" They laughed and giggled.

Except Piglet.

"Help!" he cried as he fell off.

When they got
to the bottom of the hill,
Piglet was missing.

16

"I hope Piglet is all right,"
said Pooh.

"He's still halfway up," said Roo.

17

Everyone climbed up the hill.
"Piglet was in the wrong place,"
said Owl.

"I know," said Rabbit.

"He should ride on top."

19

Once again, everyone
piled onto the sled.
This time Piglet
sat on Rabbit's shoulders.

Down they went.

"Oh nooooo!"

yelled Piglet as he

bounced off again.

When the sled reached the bottom,
everyone looked for Piglet again.
"There he is," said Kanga.
She pointed up the hill.

Everyone climbed back up.

23

"Piglet," said Pooh,
"this time you sit
at the very front."

Piglet sat in front of Roo.

Roo held on to Piglet.

Down, down they went,
fast as the wind.
Roo was having so much fun
that he waved his arms
in the air—
and out Piglet fell.

Once more, everyone climbed
back up the hill to Piglet.
Piglet sighed and said,
"I'm too small to sled,
so I'll just watch.
But thank you for trying."

Christopher Robin spoke up.

"I have an idea," he said.

"You sit in the middle.
And we'll all hold on to you,
so you can't bounce off."

Everyone piled onto the sled.
Piglet held on tight to
Christopher Robin.

Pooh held on tight to Piglet.
Everyone else made sure
Piglet couldn't bounce off.

Down, down they went!
Everyone laughed and giggled,
Piglet the loudest!

Can you match the words with the

pictures?

tree

sled

boots

Piglet

Owl

Fill in the missing letters.

t_il

P_oh

sca_f

hi_l

K_nga

Follow all the adventures
of Pooh and his friends!

Be Quiet, Pooh!

Bounce, Tigger, Bounce!

Eeyore Finds Friends

The Giving Bear

Happy Birthday, Eeyore!

Happy Valentine's Day, Pooh!

Pooh and the Storm That Sparkled

Pooh Gets Stuck

Pooh's Best Friend

Pooh's Christmas Gifts

Pooh's Easter Egg Hunt

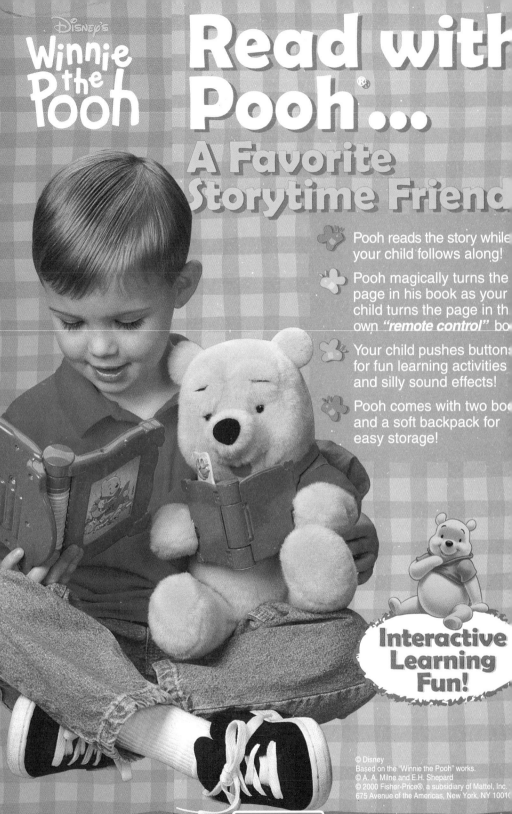